INSIGHT WIZARD

-SPECTRUM OF THOUGHTS

<u>DISCLAIMER</u>

This book is a collection of poems and our editors have made their efforts to edit the work of our co-authors.all the poems have been placed unique in this book.

We have tried our best to check for plagiarism in the writeups featured in the book.the book consists only the original writeups.

ACKNOWLEDGEMENT

The completion of this book would not have been possible without the hard work of all the co-writers and the core members of FanatiXx Publications.

A huge thanks to the core team who have given a hundred percent to this book...

Special thanks to Hitesh Hinduja for Book cover, Synopsis and the title of book.,

We would also like to thank each one of you who believed in us and brought this book...

A big thanks to all the four writers for their immense support and patience.

Above all, thanks to God and parents for blessings and love.

Contents

Rupika Teotia, an 18 year old girl , ambitious enough to climb on various obstacles in life , currently pursuing BTech in computer science from Indira Gandhi Delhi technical University for women . She likes adding feathers to her hat , by being persistent enough to do a lot in life . She likes to do dancing, singing and most importantly writing. She is now a published writer by being a part of many anthologies. Talking about this particular book, it's a dream come true for her. She had been working really hard for five years now to come at this level. Portraying several talents is not easy but is exciting for a champ like her. She aspires towards being a generous, kind and caring human being whereas wishes to make her parents proud . Her message to every parent of a daughter is "daughters are daughters, they are never intending to be your son, but by just being a daughter they can make you all proud , you just have to believe in them ".

Follow her: - @scar_of_the_wind_____

<u>BY DESTINY</u>

Namastey sahab ! He said and smiled

The eleven year old , worked a mile

He asked me for biscuits with tea

And I grinned at destiny

He was fighting with the warmth

I was getting in very tiny

I felt it all along , why is life just so hard

Even though we know the facts ,

Why we get into it ?

Even after knowing World is a trap ,

By which we all are surrounded

we get in and in by time

and by time we all are wounded

Destiny is a player

the one defeating us

and trust on luck is a gamer

every time cheating on us

INSIGHT WIZARD

we give and take

sometime this all we make

the head and tail of our lives we do

and nothing is done , nothing is really made

we feel to give up and

to leave the game someday

but the defeats all time

teach us

and thus make us ready for the next day

We get cheated , then too play

some amusement the statement behold

but we then to hay

and thus lie scattered and covered with clay

By Rupika Teotia

<u>JUSTICE</u>

I chose the shallow waters to hide

I am not interested to return to the grind

My words are heard but left aside

Is this justice , this wasn't in my mind

I am the victim , as I feel

Betrayal and breach , will I heal

I am the culprit as they say

Will I recover , or fall like clay

I am the custom they design

My words are broken , lying aside

I am the youth they define

Though I can never put up as fine

I am the beauty , they play

I am the soul , they say

I am the thirsty , they made

I wait for justice , they said.

-By Rupika Teotia

KILLED AND DIED

I saw her wailing at night

But could not console her might.

I knew she cried ,

But I knew she tried

The society concluded 'she is wrong'

I was by her side .

I know her dreams were No less

But she was the differing eye

Made to marry , made to cook

Made to learn , always shook

Made to control , made to shut

She was even tagged as slut

She was burnt , she was tied

No body , nobody even eyed.

Ultimately she died

I wish I could have gone to stop him

Stop him from attacking my daughter ,

Make her feel loved , to cherish her laughter .

I would have saved the apply of my eye .

But ultimately they killed her ,and I let her die

By Rupika Teotia

NOISES UNHEARD

The noises in deep hearts of people
That lack being heard
I seem to listen to the screams
Those are rarely heard
I have seen them crying and wailing in pain
They just want to ask
That by doing such an offence
What are we trying to gain?

We loose people due to wars
We kill some to win the chores
Filling their place is next to impossible
But we overlook these things and
Try being practical
Being practical is not in vain
But don't be emotionless
The time always comes back
There is no till no less

We lack listening the noises because they create a silence
This silence created by bombs, missiles and nuc's
This silence silences
We being happy overshadow other's pain
And then we think again and again
That why, we are not having any gain

This loss created in never to be filled
The death can never to be killed
But try being avoiding

INSIGHT WIZARD

Not with real things
But with noises
These noises of wars and pains of people
The screams and mournings
Over the death of brave soldiers
We forget our patriotism otherwise
But just don't overlook try being wise
Just try being wise

By Rupika Teotia

MYSTERY

That gloom in their eyes

Made me feel guilty

Yet they offered hatred

And u was a mystery

That honour made them kill me

But my brothers became glorified .

And I became a mystery

They buried me in the fields

Because I had the courage to fly free

They shot me in the heart

My blood went through

My love falling apart

And that fail had no clue

They didn't even sniff once

Before choking mg soul

Ironically I tied then Rakhi to protect my whole

Because I loved him

I was murdered brutally

Was it a fault , or just my destiny?

My mother didn't wail once

I wish I could hug her tons .

My guilt was yet greater

Than they could have thought

But their actions made me distraught .

I loved them all , but could disagree .

And thankfully they set me free.

By Rupika Teotia

FREEDOM

Mountains and seas, the early divine

Varied religions , but still aligned

Diverse but unite , is why we shine

Glory and victory are all the signs

They fleet away to let us fly

They gave us wings to touch the sky

Sacrifices are varied , the corpses they carried

They showed the skills and power to be free

They said " no terms to be accepted, we won't agree" .

Fought for us , made us flee

But never did demand any fee .

The motherland *India* , gave birth to vigorous stalwarts

They left their home and all the comforts

Lives in seas and in deserts

They were our army, our saviours

But we have lost , the glory they gave

No patriotism , just defame

INSIGHT WIZARD

Rights are earned and fought for

But beds are longed now more and more

Seven exceptions,

yet freedom to speak

Liars politicians , population is so sleek

Out of demands , no choices behold

But yet we have the freedom to choose .

Baseless bondages ,

yet freedom to live.

Poor people , forget and forgive .

Poison polluted air ,

yet freedom to breathe.

Carefully curated censored content,

Yet freedom to read .

By Rupika Teotia

<u>LIFE</u>

An unsolved mystery
With highs and lows
But nobody knows
Where to go

A site of affection and lots of care
It gives everything which nobody dare
Reaching the highs and knowing the lows
Can help you learn the way to sow
New seeds with love and nourishing them
Caring like a child and growing with them

An instance of expectations and pressure
Can lead to high promotions
We all know how to deal with what
But gives some time to heal each slot

Yes, this is life full of
Instances of expectations and pressure
Site of affection & lots of care
It's just an unsolved mystery
Which can never be solved
But can be lived to the fullest

Acquire this life with happiness

Not with sorrow &sadness

If want to be great

Live as much as you can with various traits

Get good knowledge and habits too

Then you will earn the art of living

Not just saying 'I live it too'

By Rupika Teotia

<u>LIFE WE SEE</u>

The Complications we see
Nobody could even plea
The life is bound to me
But the world is surrounded by sea

The sea of love and care
The sea of affection , don't you dare
Dare not to spread hatred
This can heal u but not the masses

The people who die, never complain
They accept their destiny and follow the same
The one's who live, seems in pain
As their think their efforts go in vain

Some see the extremes
Sill some are mediocre
The one's seeming rich, sometimes turn to ditch
the left are the poor ones, who don't know
What to do in terms

The life is full of ups and downs
Leave the sins and wear the crowns
The crowns of happiness will give a lot
Don't think of them just as a jot

The day u will be happy and satisfied
U will see the world's best side
Neglect the bad's, see the good's
Try wearing a hood

Love all and spread it too
The day with peace will soon come true.

By Rupika Teotia

<u>FLEE</u>

What is wrong what is right?

It is getting hard to determine

Telling others or hiding it on

Teasing others or leaving them for all

Kill them the way they did

Tell them how they fled

Let them realize the pain they gave

Which they are finding just as a thread

All flew no left

I thought they knew about the theft

That they did to me

Vanishing my thoughts

Now I feel like having a dreadful drought

Which made the feelings thirsty more

But still there are empty chores

The corners, find me

Being alone, strides me

As if I am different

But,

I wish to be as before

Just wish to fill all the chore

Should I?

Let them know what thirsty is in me

And tell them what they need not flee

Ask them that they need not flee

Ask them to stay for all

As I needed them in the way I recognize after all

By Rupika Teotia

<u>TWO HANDS</u>

Words are not said,

eyes too are in gloom

But all I know is that

my smile is for you

my happiness is with you

without you,

I am unsaid , unshown and broken

like a mirror the tears do flow ,

but all the fear

My heart is in sorrow because of the terror

The terror of losing you someday

My might will then turn into clay

to which anyone would play

Yes,my tears for you are always true

but my smile with you gives a beautiful view

The view of our bond

the image of our togetherness

The day u look and smile at me

every sin is turned into nothingness

I am confounded,

INSIGHT WIZARD

my world is surrounded

and its all of a mess

some sort of a chess

A tough game is to played

And if the king die the game is swayed

So my king is mine forever

Living in my heart till ever

But then too , hands of us I wish to join

by two hands , which we will someday coin

By Rupika Teotia

DEFEATS

World is a trap ,
we are all surrounded
Getting in and in by time
and by time we are all wounded

Destiny is a player
the one defeating us
and trust on luck is a gamer
every time cheating on us

we give and take
sometime this all we make
the head and tail of our lives we do
and nothing is done , nothing is really made

we feel to give up and
to leave the game someday
but the defeats all time
teach us
and thus make us ready for the next day

We get cheated , then too play
some amusement the statement behold
but we then to hay
and thus lie scattered and covered with clay

By Rupika Teotia

MIRROR

The clean mirror whenever I see

some gloom is visible

but never ever a plea

darkness of character

which we never see

naked eyes don't show it

but yes with eyes of practicality

we do see!

hatred of blood , despair is lost

though a cheat , but how a trust

Mirror , Oh ! mirror

A day will show people their truth

And then no mercy will fall

and there will be no pity

The promises taken are never so

seriously too

a look of lobe is never true

it's just pretended to hook

hooking feelings is done all time

and it is reported , the world is shook

INSIGHT WIZARD

shaken heads and shaken minds

the poor mirror shows face but not our might.

By Rupika Teotia

<u>BLIND OUTRAGE</u>

The outrage on roads

The stone pelters were thrashing us down

We were there to protect all of us

But still were in need of our lives .

All the deep thoughts , all the Jai Hinds

We were striving each second

To derive out justice

But was it fair to attack us ?

Do we deserve that ?

I was , 2000km ,away from my home .

Was trying to protect our people from this storm

Yet , I was abandoned

Yet , I got blackened

Was that justified ?

Isn't this horrifying ?

I was each breathe of mine falling

Yet I was scrawling .

I knew they will kill us ,

But it was my duty to remain just .

INSIGHT WIZARD

I strived harder to pull out victory .

That bullet shot my destiny

I wish the crowd protected us

I wish as I served the nation .

It could stay just , maybe it's only my imagination

By Rupika Teotia

INSIGHT WIZARD

AIL IT TODAY

The ailing planet ,seeking for ail

due to our activities ,getting more &more pail

punished by us and we lest feel

being getting hurt and badly needs heal

choking the drains

the waste we through

chokin the throats

the things we let flow and blow in air

with most carelessness

when comes to us back we feel a bit tensed

but then we are back & again careless

its our home need some care

don't hurt it more don't even dare

else if it will come to punish us

it will not forbid our sins

caught we are badly in development trends

but lest feel anything about the dense

the dense forest we cut

the dense river we drought

and the dense air much pure

INSIGHT WIZARD

but these all now are lost

coming to others can't heal the cause

do it yourself and save the thoughts

save it now or will be never before

please find a way to fill the chores

or let us die

just like never before

By Rupika Teotia

STORY OF A CHILD LABOUR

My body was torn , I was crying loudly

My friends were almost dead , they were screaming sadly

We were tired , we were harmed

They were harassing us

And we stayed calm

Those bricks were heavy , then those books

I would carry , those notebooks

Those plenty of smiles and folks in uniforms

They stared me , and scared me from their forms

I was abide , but never recognised

I was living , but never alive

Those breaths made me carry those loads to build homes .

Those opened eyes signified ,I am living

That tea stall I remember ,

My master their was no less than a monster

He scolded me for nothing

I hardly ate anything

Those empty stomach , those glittery eyes

Were never forbidden

Never alive

I cried in anger , I want to die

But then my sister smiled , you are the only living eye

You are the one who can make us stay alive

You can help me educate , please don't die .

Please don't die .

By Rupika Teotia

<u>ABANDONED MILES</u>

Abandoned smiles , preaching of love

care offered to everyone

no fake emotions , just true guts

and here comes the sand of demotions

keeping aside the fears he flew

leaving behind the ones he knew

for the betterment of people along

he knows it all, everything he knew

love presented to all the souls

left behind in all the moulds

the man of unity , the man of innocence

the man of smiles and condolence

keeping away tensions ,

never minding nothing he mentions

that's how he lives his life

the king always walks alone in miles

By Rupika Teotia

<u>WRONG</u>

Doors are shut, lights are closed

darkness besides me

making me more tore

words are deep, sea is sore

salt is filled, all in the chore

Abusing my feeling,

making me wrong

want to sit idol and all alone

mind is working but thoughts are gone

nothing seems my in, but all is on

understanding my perception

but telling me I am mad

these words hurt even more

but are said to me, thus I am glad

my sins are mine but tears are yours

all these are better said but never felt

INSIGHT WIZARD

my tears are mine

my cries are sign

my broken heart life

but no one to hug and cry

By Rupika Teotia

Hailing from a small city Malda, West Bengal, Suchismita dreams high to touch the sky. She is an avid reader, writer, poet, muser, scribbler, storyteller, published author, blogger, nature lover, social worker & a freelance model. She will soon complete her graduation in Zoology. She has also completed her advanced diploma in Computer Application. She has authored more than 100 anthologies as a co-author, most of them are in process of publication. Her debut book titled "Fields of Sonnet" will soon be launched.

She aspires to become a great author & heal people through her words' majesty in the future. She is available on her instagram account @storytellersuchismita & her email id - ghoshalsuchismita019@gmail.com

I SEE FREEDOM IN LIGHTS -

Once the darkness concluded

Its journey, just here in my heart,

In my mind,

In my soul,

I saw the bondage got smeared &

Freedom canoodling my body.

Slowly yet balancedly,

My room was getting filled with lights,

Lights of hope,

Lights of care,

Lights of small satisfaction.

The way once I stumbled upon

On an unmoving tragedy,

& got flooded with blood;

Frozen shivers, procrastinating journey,

Flashbacks tormented, pricked & omitted my entity.

A living corpse, shrieked & gambled on life,

Now giggling in flourishing shyness,

Playing the game of love.

Lights tempting my soul's aura,

INSIGHT WIZARD

Murks deemed, Rainbow illuminated,

I have found freedom in lights,

Murmuring lullabies of divinity

& tethering my soul with extreme tenacity.

~ ©*storytellersuchismita*

CYCLICAL PAIN ▪

My pain is cyclical,

Reverberates jingles of tears,

Lonely in a sea shore,

Galloping the rush of curly waves,

& measuring those numerous numbers

By comparing with my stormy pain.

Recalling the enormous failure that,

How many times I failed,

Failed to describe them with a buried mind & a stitched
mouth,

Failed to make them surmise

The elongated procedure of swallowing the blood

& again spewing the terrors of death.

Here on a hollow world,

People are too self-centric to carefully pause & look,

& understand their hollow brain full of broken thoughts.

Pain is the universal truth,

Touches everyone's lips;

Some fear to show the stains of heavy love-making,

Some blatantly chew it,

Some are stuck & oscillating between these two sharp end,

INSIGHT WIZARD

Just the way I am!

Arrogant convictions tightly pressed

In the deepest corner of my mind,

I tried utmost,

To flee away from them,

To eyewash them from clogging me;

But no, I surrendered after a blunder

& they cyclically came like a bunch of happy buds.

Their motive ,- only to destroy, only to foil me up,

Whereas the rest cruel world frowned

& enjoyed the concert of my brutal destruction.

I hated, hate & shall be hating to be loud & shriek,

My anguishes will never stay in brief,

Will be licking my body thoroughly

But I won't reveal the recurring pain's evil sound

Burying the melody of my mind in a stiff ground.

~©*storytellersuchismita*

NEGLIGENCE

Citylights in the early morning,

Seem quite like the exaggerated dots,

Trying to push a little bit more to be prominent,

Amidst thousands of other protruding dark sources.

Me, standing on the balcony slightly bending

My upper part of the body,

Resting my elbow on the relling.

Insomniac nights & rapidly increasing time,

I sing lullabies of cacophony.

A tint of smoke disturbes my mind,

& Distraction leads me to the alley of withdrawal syndrome;

A syndrome of lynching memories,

A syndrome of never to be valued,

A syndrome of unnumbered negligence.

Days & paths look like an unending journey,

Which I am forced to oblige,

Chanting the names I once prioritized

& got a sequence of rejections followed by

Unseen texts, unreplied calls & unwanted humiliation.

I pleaded sitting down on my knees,

INSIGHT WIZARD

Carrying my unfurled heart in front of them,

But all in vain , as they threw it like a flushable waste.

Negligence is nothing but a lump stuck in throat,

Pricking the mind, resulting in a severe sore ;

Now, burning utmost with the cigars of barratry,

I set the gates of my hearts in fire

To enfold my soul in a cemetery.

~©*storytellersuchismita*

LOVE FEELS LIKE CIGARS

Love feels like two cigars

Slowly blazing for a smooth destruction,

Exhaling the black smoke ,

Consisted of misconception

Stirred with immense care,

& inhaling the mystery called ecstasy & lust.

Enticing beauty which I see, you saw & they will see

Will soon be transformed into a gigantic trap,

Or an illusional canal full of problems

That previously gives the vibes

Of sharing bed in comfort,

The comfort of roses & the comfort of fragrant petals.

Life runs on a symmetry,

Aiming to be concealed by two loving arms,

& here, the love comes

INSIGHT WIZARD

Disguising like a healing aid,

Like a sanjeevani ambrosia

Or, quite like a turning point in life.

But, little does everyone know

Behind every divine creature,

There lies a strong addiction leading towards death,

Endangered yet peaceful.

It's ironic as we are addicted to cigars

But they have to finish at the end

Like a mourning good-bye hug

Sharing us the euphoria of attachment

& drawing tears, only to be lost & crowned

At the same time.

~ *©storytellersuchismita*

STARS MADE THROUGH FRIENDSHIP

Stars aren't made overnight,

Going through every storm & thunders

Proves how much they put themselves

To glitter like stars in friendship.

Hands in hands, they proved themselves

To be the strongest companions,

Two hearts ,situated in different bodies

Yet united for lifetime, shows

How intensely they hold each other's soul.

Happy faces hide stories behind the curtain,

Freedom leads a source full of massacres,

& an unbreakable bond too tells a story of

Thousand fights, misunderstandings & secret love.

Friendship is a gem whereas

The persons behind are the gemstones.

Some play a role of ruby,

Some emerald, & some pearls.

But all are found, gathered

In the extreme bottom of a sea

INSIGHT WIZARD

Empowering their own world with their own happiness;

By the passage of time they come upside

With the curvaceous waves

& unfurl themselves from their shell

Just like a true friendship unfurls its true colour.

A firm & feathered love,

Traced in a home called friendship

Leads us to nowhere but

A place full of honest swears

& paradisiacal bondings,

A soil with strong hold & firm base

Enfolded by doubtless loyalty.

Stars, made over the years

Slowly covering our full entity

Giving extreme exuberation & friendship.

~ *©storytellersuchismita*

DIARY EXHILARATES MY SOUL

I'm a fragrant lover,

Not the foreign made expensive colognes ,

But the ones my diaries have.

I scribble all the day

Sensing the different flavours

Embedded in each of my writings,

& sniffing the essence they spread

Through the pages of my diary.

Some poems yet to be revealed,

Some stories yet to be read

& some tales yet to be told,

I find their ensuing entity hidden

In every undisclosed lines.

My soul feels a peculiar exhilaration

With the love they own

& with the exuberant vibes they portray,

Secretly gets applause from my heart.

Canoodling the letters with my lips,

Adoring them with the tips of my fingers,

INSIGHT WIZARD

I get nothing exclusive more than my diary.

The way it encircles me all the time,

From the lazy mornings to the late night sobs,

Is something found after ages.

So many unknown yearnings

Engraved confidentially in the yellow pages

Vanquishing those impeachments sealed by others;

So many wrong- doings & mistaken shenanigans

Are forgiven by my words in a grandeur way.

Diary is a true exhilator, imbibing my soul

& I, being a pious art-lover

Devoted my entity to my diary.

~ ©storytellersuchismita

FREEDOM VS UNFREEDOM

Alluring,

Astonishing, Amazing,

Bewitching, Enticing, Enthralling,

Freedom can't be described through the adjectives

Or portrayed by heavy compliments…

Neither it can be touched nor can be seen..

But can be sensed through your heart

& felt by your soul.

How much you will learn, grow, imply & earn

Are the sources of real freedom.

The way you will speak, behave, love, work & think

Are the paths to enlightenment & then freedom.

Freedom kisses & recovers your soul

& you let your soul knelt down in front of freedom's beauty.

Annihilating

Amorphous, Abashing,

Bewildering, Ensnaring, Endangering,

Unfreedom doesn't ask for your consent

To get showcased in front of a broad daylight…

Neither it sensizes your mind nor mercies you..

It can only ride on your veins & chock your throat

& bind your entity till you exhale your last breath.

How much you will be enraged, destroy, demolish & loss

Are the ways your unfreedom embodies.

How much you will be indecent, arrogant, harmful &
terrifying

Are the paths lead you to darkness & then unfreedom.

Unfreedom snatches your enkindling education

& you let your soul entrapped in the abyss of unfreedom's
slavery.

~ ©*storytellersuchismita*

<u>RAINBOW OF THOUGHTS</u>

The simultaneous thoughts

Which my brain draws like a draft

With charcoal pencils,

Come out as rainbows directly on my diary.

They colour my heart, my mind

& extra colours stain my soul after

Leaking out from the pages.

Running fast from the fears,

Fears of love, lies & destruction,

I caught the hands of my poetry.

They never disappointed me

Rather concocted my life

& every event got syllably decorated

Through the scribbles.

Rainbows are happy beings,

Colour the colourless &,

INSIGHT WIZARD

Fulfill a person's dream.

My thoughts endeavour a new way of living

With the helping hand of my verses.

Inescapable teardrops breakout in a pool of glooms,

When the rainbow of my thoughts

Drenches me until the extreme point of pacification,

Cures my inner wounds ,

& instant colour bring freshness

Being the vibrant angel of heaven.

~©storytellersuchismita

WHEN SMILE COVERS THE INNER THOUGHTS

When mouth is numb, excessively inedible,

After a thousand genuflection, fails to surmise,

Fails in vain & surrenders before my pen;

My words win, express all the unexpressed.

When my smile shields my inner thoughts

Secretly grieving for the lost peace,

& persuades for the pacification of mind,

Hands over the responsibility on my pen;

My pen happily receives all the work on its shoulders

& carries out all of it with utmost sincerity.

Words, verses, poems & lyrics

Are synonymous with my soul's expression.

Years after years, decades after decades,

Nomads find the lost solace in words' grace

Just like my lonely being found the elation in poetry.

After crossing odds, riding on the struggles,

I reached the place where only my soul is valued,

I reached here to the world of scribbles

& traced my happiness along with my love.

INSIGHT WIZARD

When smile covers the inner thoughts,

My soul talks through the yellow pages of my diary,

When nothing fails to heal my wounds,

My words works as a medicinal cure to my soul.

~ ©*storytellersuchismita*

DON'T THINK ME A VAGABOND

Don't think me vagabond

At any cost for anyone's sake,

I only chose to show my benevolence,

I only cared to flourish my kindness,

I only thought of loving you unconditionally,

I only spoke everybit of my concern for you,

But never portrayed my enclosed side,

That side which knows no mercy,

Splinters your ego & splashes water on your flame,

Twists your evil purposes & throws you on a trash.

Don't think me a worthless creature,

In a world full of masked faces,

Till you preferred to play the love-game,

I trusted & only received broken pieces,

Till you caressed my tufts of hair,

I surrender before your tempting aura,

INSIGHT WIZARD

& till you laughed behind my back &

Accomplished a good act,

I already sacrificed my entire soul to you.

Now like a duty to be finished,

You finished my chapter & chewed all of it,

Don't defame my name calling me a "vagabond" now,

If my enraged soul burst like a volcano,

Turning you into ashes

Won't be delayed till my 2nd thought.

~ ©*storytellersuchismita*

<u>LOVE OF MY LIFE</u>

Arrogantly she called for my name,

Bewitching was her voice from a distance

Confused was my mind,

As she was the only love of my life.

Bestowing my every bit of love, I

Concreted the base of bond with my own hands.

Adorned like a princess of my dream,

Beguilingly she smiled & slowly came forward,

Conquered my thirst to see her at a glance.

Afterall when I proceeded to touch & love,

Benevolently she receded nodding her head,

Consoling my soul it was all an illusion!

Alas! It was all a dream,

Bereaved me , at last got my senses back,

Conjuring was the whole drama & I lost all the track!

~ *©storytellersuchismita*

SOCIAL MEDIA TURNED ME LANGUID

Anguishes are all over here,

& Social media being the dragon

Spitting fires & fueling situations.

How a small thing turns abruptly

Into a big issue & ready to trample us!

How much a person is insecure

When a post pops up on our cell phone screen,

& spots how a dark skin, a fat body, a lean structure

Or a distorted body part , a dwarf & a very tall

Can easily be endemic of extreme bully & laughter!

How much a social issue is picked simultaneously

& makes everyone fighters with ever-typing fingers!

How much a girl or a boy is easy available

Counted on the basis of a randomly posted picture

Engaging their personal life!

How much a person is a live sex-toy

Rated for the elated eyes to arouse their sensation

Licking their revealed skin with eyeballs!

How much we've been wavering

Between two walls & stoning a human inch by inch

INSIGHT WIZARD

Counted with increased mentions of Hindus or non hindus,

Muslims or non Muslims, Minors or majors,

Outsiders or insiders, bhakts or non-bhakts etc!

Homes are not home to the random public,

They find solace homing all the social media platforms,

Facebook, instagram, twitter & others,

Fights & debates turn into a massacre ,

Ten times faster than the rapidly declining humanity.

Everyone & everything is a prey of social predators,

Opaque problems, yet solutions are ever-visible

As eye-washed humans belong from social media.

Outskirts of over smartness is stained with chauvin,

People are ever-ready to outsmart anyone,

Even a tea cup is judged with a cup of coffee here.

Life is a mess, a prominent garbage of websites &

Their stinky waste, crushed with a little bit of distortion.

I've been turned into a hopeless fellow,

Fearing the flaws they are craving to get,

I've been turned into something called languid;

My limbs are not equally functional,

Langourness has wrapped me like a flue,

& I never am efforting to unravel my soul.

INSIGHT WIZARD

What's the gain, what's the ecstasy, what's the divinity

To stay in a social trap full of foul gestures & obscenity?

I hate it now, more than the lovers increasing in a second,

I hate to be a slave in unfreedom,

I loathe on being puppets of fake socialism

In the era of illiberal social media.

What's left in being boiled to this hell's liquid?

Social media has turned me a full-fledged languid!

~ ©storytellersuchismita

<u>LOVE</u>

Alluring,

Bewitching, bewildering,

Conjuring, confound & conclusion.

Amazing, awe-striking,

Benevolence, benignity, bedazzling,

Confidence, capability, courageous & comforting.

Astonishing, awesome, angelic,

Bodacious, bonny, balanced, bliss,

Candascent, courteous, charming, creative & credible.

Love is everything which pleases your soul,

& your soul forms in the point where love resides.

~ *©storytellersuchismita*

I SPY

I spy,

Spy on you ,

Spy on you day & night,

Spy on you all the minutes & seconds,

Spy on you for all the hours,minutes & seconds,

Spy on you by the mirror,

Spy on you by the mirror of my heart,

Spy on you every now & then,

Spy on you for I never can forget your image,

Spy on you for my soul are glued,

Spy on you for my glued soul craves for you,

Spy on you to never miss you,

Spy on you for a slight glance of sightless you,

Spy on you for you are indelibly irresistible,

Spy on you for the indelible you can feel my untold love.

~ *©storytellersuchismita*

PRONE TO GOD

What if one day you wake up from a dream

Finding yourself in a trunk full of trash,

& then vultures speed up to relishingly eat you?

Won't you be frightened & start quivering

& your fingers, magnetized, initiate counting

Your curses automatically?

Your luck bursts out in laughter,

For how it injected fear in your veins overnight!

Humans now-a-days are no more humans

They are empty saucers

Prone to catch sticky ketch-up of vices.

Don't you think your soul is too in surveillance

Of the almighty supreme soul?

High time to change our inner obscenity & evils;

Hatred leads you to nowhere but a dark hole

Jammed by all the poisonous insects.

Why the good terms seem foul to you

When evil habits made you nothing but a piece of shit?

Remember a massive sixer hit you hard

INSIGHT WIZARD

When you were just a four inch of seven years

& you cried hard running directly to your mother?

What changed, what exactly turned wrong in a decade

As you stopped going to her & tell your concerns?

Nothing changed as only you've chosen to be beaten!

Illusions never destine you to the path of illumination,

& enslavement never gives you

The solace of enchantment.

Stop your cravings for the odds

Where everything gets a last bite named "Death",

& start choosing the destiny

Where humans are prone to the goods & lastly to 'God'.

~ ©storytellersuchismita

Priyadarshini Sahu is from Bhubaneswar, Odisha. She was born on 2nd December 1997. Currently she is pursuing M.sc (Plant Breeding and Genetics). Apart from being a meritorious student she is an avid dancer, writer, poet and foodie. She believes in herself the most as she has seen many rough times at a young age, leading her to attempt suicides and has now stood up strong. For her, fighting is more important than winning. Persevere and you will one day obviously succeed. Find friends to share pain, you may count your pen in too.

Follow her:-

Instagram: - silent_volcano212

I LIVE, TO ACHIEVE DEATH

Things ebbing out at the face of death

Is menancingly awesome to me.

Can't I just leach 'Death' out?

No, it always drizzles life.

Meaningless relations stay not to fatigue

Medicines dissolve out too,

Money will buy the death certificate

Yet I won't be the one to strive.

The pink I chose over blue

Will all turn white at the grave,

Three yards of dirt and ash,

And the manner too, of washing my chive(s).

Your call will not wake me anymore,

Nor you blasting your donkey voice,

INSIGHT WIZARD

Save only good memories of me,

For I'll return. I believe.

73

- Silent Volcano
@silent_volcano212

TOO GODLY TO BE TRUE

There's a hey and ho in me, also a hey no ni no

Butchered by a hammer with a sober socialized glow.

Hush, don't make me cry

Tears that wait till eternity to fall and dry.

I wanna be the Hercules I pretend.

Positive vibes are all that I must send.

No, I'm no human, I'm God.

Why don't you just kneel before the lord?

Eyes that bleed onto pillows every night,

With a divine twinkle are next morning sight.

You caught me hiding it,

You made the rule, I'm just abiding (by) it.

I'm too scared I might disappoint you.

I choose to be an iceberg and smile in lieu.

Amidst breath that smells of frustration,

Biceps that sum up perspiration;

Dent over nose numbering my years,

Lips that have practiced to hide tears,

I live a life of complete fake;

Yet to confess, I tremble and shake:-

I am just a mistaken identity

Mostly for an expected version of me.

75

- Silent Volcano

THE RUSH

You hit hard under my belt

Yes against law, yet

I sat oozing blood from all

Of my orifices.

O That bitter curry you made

The one that I gulped down

A grin bubbled up right from my stomach

I clenched my oesophagus and broadened my lips

Just to please you.

Nevertheless you were bent on pushing me

Over the tumbler brim

I couldn't contain myself, how

Would have you too?

Slowly I started losing me,

Your blows making me more blue...

Blue, I am, mentally and under the eye.

Red on the inside now, you strike,

I bend as you curve me.

Yielding to your forces, I'm exhausted.

Slow and steady, still i lost;

INSIGHT WIZARD

Unwantingly, yet, vehemently;

I now want you, at any cost.

- Silent Volcano

I WON

How hard for me has it been

None the less you can imagine ...

The best, the worst, the least expected...

But I have bled to be serene.

My life's worth more than the cuts

You put salt to, with tattered and

A bloodied body full of ifs and buts,

I fight in vain against the quicksand.

The divinity in me flickered at last

Plunging my soul into pitch dark.

Come on, get me a torch.

Lest the Devil beside me should lark.

I put down the sword, 'twas easier.

Atleast I'll live, though not shine,

It was not only a hard battle,

Even the body I fought against was mine.

-Silent Volcano

FIXING EYE ON I

'I' was never for 'Igloo' on slate

Took me long to realize;

'I' was the seven faced serepentine for Hercules,

A world of conflicts within me,

Still, I rise.

Busy as the bee, sad as a smiley,

Took time to figure out 'I',

Not with a chalk, but with Vivekananda eyes.

Still, I rise.

Giving in to the hammering world,

Giving out to the pestered humanity,

Drained in by waves of tears,

Drained out by the second hand.

Taking time for collecting oxygen,

Giving time for biological library to widen;

Cut and sewn never endingly into celebrity fit size,

Still, I rise.

Humming over the charvoal path,

Brightening the disparaged curriculum vitae,

INSIGHT WIZARD

Just like winter forcing to bath,

My body gets plucked, being a compositae.

Still, I rise.

Go to hell, Be down to earth,

Made me a hanging lantern;

Burning out of salary is a regular pattern.

Hand and gloves with a over-tome to loathe .

Still, I rise.

Ctrl+Alt+Deleting mistakes of others,

Shift+Increasing my manners,

Ctrl+A all the positivity

With a red bar, yeah, battery scarcity.

Still, I rise,

Till I'm wise,

And that's all to summarise.

-Silent Volcano

NEBULOUS PARLEY

"Look the moon's ogling at you!"

"Yeah, I see you staring at me."

"How can you be so handsome?"

"It's called induction, baby."

"Look how the stars shine at you!"

"GPS isn't exact too; 10cm far, are you?"

"Every charm of yours is unseconded!"

"You have none that I need to sew."

"You are my luckiest catch!"

"I'm eye-to-eye with my dream-come-true."

"Sweet, cute, caring."

"Sweeter, cuter and daring."

"Words fall short for your description."

"You are above words, there's no suspicion."

"I'm falling for you again."

"I'm trying not to do that, but in vain."

"Come hither, show me your heart."

"Choosing a mirror, rather, would be smart."

"Let's rest, you might be tired."

INSIGHT WIZARD

"You are my coffee, the strongest brew."

"You are the best in the world,yaar!!"

"My world is spelt y-o-u."

83

- Silent Volcano

TACITE MOT

Some secrets will get cremated with me,

Some; that will never grow into sod.

Some tear soaked nights will sleep

And some smiles might cry bedore the Lord.

Deeds of idiocy outweigh that of kindness,

Few masks of mine and foundation of others,

Shame that on times feels heavy on my tongue;

I will watch them while my earthly body smoulders.

Speciality that I know of, yet not boast,

Attention that I crave,not deserve;

Dreams that I worship, not follow;

Memories that I wanted but couldn't preserve.

Pain that I ignore to be forte,

Happiness ignored in fear of jealousy,

Some hidden jumbled pieces of my soul

And the whole of my nib's balladry.

-Silent Volcano

<u>MARRIED, NOT ENSLAVEN</u>

Chairman may change to chairperson,

Nevertheless, you remain just veiled cooks.

Family doesn't have a place for you;

Find some in the 'chardibari' nooks.

Once crimson coloured your forehead,

Black coloured your life.

You were not ever a human,

You were a daughter and now a wife.

Your husband may do heroin,

You are to take chulah fumes and burns;

You presumed you were important?

Did you pass your name to your sons?

You worship your in-laws,

And your in-laws, theeir daughter;

You weigh as much of your dowry,

And the darker you are, the lesser.

Get a hold of yourself, lady;

You breathe oxygen, they do too.

Nine months are favours, not duty;

Thrive like the humane you are,

Takc all you should, don't ask;

'Cause one thing you must cherish is YOU.

-Silent Volcano

<u>SHE'S DIFFERENT</u>

I met her over a coffee,

Roasted to be specific, unlike mine.

3 tsp sugars for me,

'Unsweetened' did her mouth shine.

(Ah, I'm sweet. She's rude.)

She pointed to the switched off router,

But the cashier looked more handsome.

Sigh! She talked me out of my break up,

Lest, should I be numb.

(May be she is.)

We, 2 tributaries, yet best friends,

One myself, and the other my earthing,

She smacks me to reality,

And poses as my elder sibling.

(Yup, just poeses.)

She's chatted everyday since,

Save when I was unconscious.

She poured slang for my carelessness, &

Hid butter under roasted coffee. 'twas obvious.

(How I want to do that!)

She has stayed so long now,

I can call her my sister technically,

Still I loathe to say, ugh,

She is just my alter ego, medically.

(She's different, right?)

-Silent Volcano

HOW TO COOK A POEM

Decide what to cook, and
Assemble the required,
Chop the main theme into
Paragraphs that are rhythm-sized.

Wash the grammar and keep aside.
Heat up the first line.
Put generous amount of flow to it.
Fry the grammar till it does shine.

As soon as the grammar's poetic,
Sprinkle some punctuation.
Let it cook till it suffices you,
Lest the diner should have dissatisfaction.

Add the main ingredient,
Simmer and change the pace.
Add more rhythm if required,
And the remaining word flakes.

INSIGHT WIZARD

Now's the time for 'cream of the poem',

All's well that ends well,

Plate on a good platform, not your diary.

To grow, you should break your shell.

Take a read-test and correct,

Leave none to blame,

Top with a fresh title leaf and

Serve with your pen name.

-Silent Volcano

A 26 year old HITESH HINDUJA living in the beautiful city of Kutch district in state of Gujarat. He reflects a varied personality including ambition, and the qualities of generosity and thoughtfulness. He encourage people for fighting what they desire and he is more about exploring things, a vast perception of how everything actually works, and such basic quality, that made him think in details about surroundings, a different point of view is must for having a unique personality and more of it he like to explore what's behind the scenes. Being involved in a family business he also have worked on different platforms in many fields, and currently working in an engineering company as an HR and Company Representative, he have been a ghost writer for many years and yet after decided to showcase his piece of arts mixed with emotions on paper. He write about those are common scenarios everyone encounters sooner or later. Since they seem so easy to write, they can quickly become a trap though; trust me. A poet perception towards the things and skills of makings emotions rhyme is next level. And finally he published his few works in 3-4 anthologies. His love for learning different things at different level makes him more efficient in them. Helping people around in many ways, finding out fun in darks, also blessed with the skills of logo designing and drawing and management, and also love to work for noble cause. With the definitive goal of becoming successful in writing, the hobby he is passionate about he is now here giving himself a chance by participating in this book and contributing his beautiful pieces with great support of other three writers…

Always up for listening to you: - dj4hinduja@gmail.com

Follow him on instagram: - poet_trees93 and men_behindthescene

<u>PRICE I PAID</u>

The price that I paid,

For keeping my honesty alive,

In the ocean of pride, I took a deep dive,

No one wants me to come out alive,

I somehow managed to survive,

A lot have been sacrificed,

To keep my honesty alive,

Look into my eyes, can you see fire inside?

Certain changes happened that's wasn't even derived,

Persons probably change in their good times,

They was concerned about you much,

Till the date they have achieved enough,

Strangers seems to be more genuine and nice,

Than someone known who left you in hard times,

The long stories that we shared all night,

That hapie moments and fake fights,

How you just forget everything, and don't even realize,

I do think sometimes,

I kept a expensive thing, i.e. my honesty alive,

But then I find myself hapie, in absence of you,

I'm tired of going through same things for long time,

Living in the dark, I need a little sunshine,

I still have respect for you inside,

But I don't need you back in my life,

The price that I paid,

For keeping my honesty alive…

-Hitesh Hinduja.

NEED A LITTLE BREAK

Oh I need a little break! From this undeserved pain,

All seems to be black, In these dark shadow and rains,

There's a lot to a day,

I have lost many mains,

I earned my pride,

The great price has been paid,

I'm different and I'm not ashamed,

I'm proud for all that I have gained,

Box full of colors, I'm a different shade,

How do you classify my grade?

I'm not just a color, indeed an emotional paint,

Leave me once for something,

And don't expect me again.

I believe in keeping bonds,

And will try to always be the same,

The change is a slow process I know,

I will change only to upgrade,

Path of truth has a lot to be faced,

It's like traveling in lonely lane.

Oh I need a little break!

From this undeserved pain,

It's hard to be left alone,

Lose the things you think you own,

Something is dead inside of me,

I don't care much you can see,

But I still miss the bond we shared,

Was it just fake love and care?

What makes me think like this?

You damaged me the way that can't be fixed.

All the things you said, I feel that all in my veins,

Oh I need a little break! From this undeserved pain.

-Hitesh Hinduja.

MOTION OF INFORMATION

Keep the right information in motion,

Add more peace to nation,

A whole group of invasion,

In the culture of inovasion,

The world is leading towards separation,

How will we find a destination,

We arent looking for any deduction,

Indeed stand together for transformation,

The power filled with seduction,

Humanity is waiting at some point of intersection,

Do the good work, keep positive motivation,

think about, choose right admisnistration,

Have some faith keep some patients,

Build a way or devote the destruction,

All that comes up is a perception,

Keep the right information in motion,

Add more peace to nation…

-Hitesh Hinduja.

<u>WORTHY LESSONS</u>

I don't need you anymore,

Heart is hard from the core,

All the stains you pour,

The invisible mask you wore,

Veins getting little sore,

How long would I be able to hold?

I don't want to lose my bold,

Though I believed the lies you told,

It was brass I assumed it as gold,

Love for you is never getting old,

I just need a new mould,

Shape my life that can stroll,

Hating you was never my goal,

Love was been polled,

I suppose this was a mess,

A bundle of stress,

I'm hapie this happened,

For a while I was threatened,

But then I realized nothing has changed,

Life just teaches you worthy lessons…

-Hitesh Hinduja.

DARK DAYS

Dark days have their own light,

Who is wrong? and who is right?

Who will leave you? Who will stand by your side?

Who will close the door? who's heart will remain open wide?

These days set the clear vision in your eyes,

Dark days have own light …

A lot had happened, a lot will,

Focus on hapie things in life,

One day everything will be superfine,

All the bad things will be left behind.,

Dark days have own light …

Revenge for bad or appreciate the right,

Know the difference and choose wise.,

The world is full of beautiful lies,

Be the fire in the box full of ice,

Dark days have own light …

Changing faces need to be recogonized.,

Confusions within are real fight,

Somethings will start to fade,

Let them go out of your sight,

Sun have to go down, look for the moon rise,

Dark days have own light …

-*Hitesh Hinduja.*

<u>JUSTICE DENIED</u>

Come let's take a break,

Discuss about upcoming fate,

Like the level of justice around,

Basic morals of justice is lying in lost and found,

Rationality In laws can now be easily found,

Equity of administration needs some rights,

People want protection while fighting with lives,

Survival being hell to describe,

Need to redirect the theories with time,

The concepts and guidelines has been forged,

Wrongs viewpoints have been formed,

Consequences of systems is damaging action of choice,

Nature of justice is probably not acting wise,

Justice now being a subject of deep philosophy,

Key elements of talents has merged towards loss,

In the show of politics and punishing the wrong,

Everyone is singing the same song,

Without a knowledge bringing monopoly along,

People don't tend to understand the management,

We are leading towards the end,

INSIGHT WIZARD

Justice will no longer be a feature,

Humanity will lose its leisure,

Still we have a little fissure,

Claim it before it's long gone,

Stop singing the same song…

-Hitesh Hinduja.

DON'T MIND

Looking at the hungry face,

I'm thinking about justice rate (ratio),

Some people are living in sun,

And some left empires abandon,

Some acts do thunder my soul,

Like that little underage child working alone,

To this beautiful world he is unknown,

Who is supposed to be blamed?

Will he ever get some grace?

Or is he running in never ending race,

He is like puppet playing his role,

Humanity somewhere has lost its goal,

I don't criticize the rich for having much,

Nor do I force them to donate,

Just take a deep look in shattered lives,

The dead hope they carry in their eyes,

We order pizza that's large in size,

Some are still begging for a bowl of rice,

We need not to sympathize,

INSIGHT WIZARD

This must stop in upcoming time,

Y don't we just act a little wise,

Y don't we think about it twice,

Again it's not about giving much,

But it does need your attention,

Help the one, who need it,

Do them justice and be kind,

I hope you don't mind…

-Hitesh Hinduja.

TOWARDS ACHIEVEMENT

What are you looking for?

Are you getting a second thought?

Wait wait wait is it about what's going on,

Isn't it the same that you planned?

Everywhere around is dark clouds and rain,

If it's not correct don't blame,

It's you, who have to stand up,

Against everything that's corrupt,

Justice nowadays catching rust,

Go on human there's a lot to come,

Bring the change you are the one,

Forget about whatever happened,

Be the brightest star, burn like sun,

Look at your dream things you haven't yet done,

It's a race between you and your soul,

Don't feel tired get up and run,

Act like a bullet be your own gun,

Life is amazing let's have little fun,

Spread some light stop feeling dull,

INSIGHT WIZARD

Don't keep on waiting at u turn,

Think about your pride and expansion,

Don't look back once you're done,

Push yourself harder towards an achievement

Do good as much as you can…

-Hitesh Hinduja.

BEHIND THE SCENES

Some of you may link to this,

But read it at your own risk,

We look hapie together I know,

But are we hapie inside,

We are into a strange figh,t

To fake something doesn't sound right,

Yes you won't be able to see sometimes,

I was losing a relation side by side,

But I have done a lot of sacrifice,

I was holding fire acting like its cube of ice,

I don't want you to judge everything,

But it's not like as you see,

Everything is different behind the scene,

Being into something makes you feel like complete,

But what when that doesn't belong to you,

What at last you will do?

You definitely have to take a step back,

Either you will die in stress,

Take a deep breath and start fresh,

Life is a journey full of surprise,

Have you played game of dice?

Then you know it's not same every time,

Just like poem isn't suppose to rhyme,

It takes a lot of me to act normal,

As same as a rock star to wear formal,

I wonder how I managed to smiled in pain,

I never loved going out in rain,

I think of me as sane,

I picked of experience that I gain,

Used a little of my brain,

We aren't together now,

That's all I want to say…

-Hitesh Hinduja.

SUPER DAD

Yes dad I wanted to tell you something,

You understand what I mean,

A lot of questions to be asked,

About the beautiful years that passed,

Can you please explain me this,

How did you managed to fulfill every wish,

Having you is living with bliss,

You worked so hard all your life,

To make our future bright,

You let me order my favorite dish,

Always there to make me feel cherish,

You make me feel like this,

That I'm born rich,

Nothing wrong in that,

Because indeed it's a fact,

I'm getting fatter, ignoring my health,

Ordering food and enjoying your wealth,

You helped me taking first steps,

Saving me from not to fall in traps,

I was being taught how to live,

All my tensions that you relieve,

Magic happens you made me believe,

My dumb shit that you connive,

Thanks for making me feel hapie inside,

It wasn't easy for you in spite,

The emotions that you hide,

To see us smile wide,

You never hostile to whatever I said,

You always kept me ahead,

I never got a chance to say you all this,

Hope you read when I get published…

-Hitesh Hinduja.

WAY YOU WANT

People don't understand the way you want,

No matter how good is your bond?

It's like living in a stage of lost and found,

I know how it sounds,

But it has made humanity shocked,

How prevailing of justice has stopped,

Act of doing nothing is caught,

Everything seems to be in blind spot,

Will we ever be able to respond?

Will we ever be able to think beyond?

Or will we always stuck in this round,

Level of living is going down,

Seems like half stuck inside the ground,

Some noise at door, can you hear the knock,

How everything around is blocked,

In a way or another we have been daunt,

Want to get out of it at any cost,

Soul inside is still at doubt,

We are being habitat living cropped,

INSIGHT WIZARD

It's all inverse as we once thought,

Somewhere inside we feel a little soft,

We somehow can't reach to the top,

We lost the fight we fought

Will you stand up again to take a shot?

To get back all that you have lost…

-Hitesh Hinduja.

<u>TICKLING CLOCKS</u>

Have you ever wonder about anything,

Like what is this all happening?

How few people are so good at singing?

How can someone stand on round wheel?

How can someone write so fine?

How we got things defined,

How opposites are combined,

And still kept aligned,

How one to another it's all bind,

Are we all somewhere linked?

Everything just change in a blink,

In the deep ocean of thoughts,

Are we all going to sink?

Let's all unite and think,

Let's decorate paper with ink,

Feel free from these social rings,

We can build our own wings,

Pull a little harder all that strings,

Let's go again to that swings,

Remember the joy it brings,

INSIGHT WIZARD

In the castle of dreams,

You are the only king,

Let go to the top of highest rock,

We are free to think outside the box,

Can you here those silent talks,

While we are on that long walks,

Look how fast is that tick tick of clocks,

We can't stay long as orthodox…

-Hitesh Hinduja.

<u>DAY IN MY DREAM</u>

I lived a day in my dream.

And it's one of amazing thing,

A day away from my phone ring,

A day without social things,

I was so hapie being just me,

A city where people wasn't mean,

A big garden that was lush green,

I lived a day in my dream…

Have you seen a magic happening?

Like birds that can literally sing,

A river that talks like human being,

A secret house built inside a tree,

A hill that has gates opening,

A flower that huge blooming,

I lived a day in my dream…

I was owner of café fiction ,

Serving people free in Christmas,

INSIGHT WIZARD

After all this was my dream business,

A nation that's free from drugs,

Children's are hapie seeing ice cream truck,

City where youngster got appropriate work,

Looking around I kept on wondering,

I lived a day in my dream…

A sky full of art,

And I was one of its parts,

All of this look little big in size,

Look the arena full of rides,

Beautiful lake always smile,

I woke up without remembering,

I lived a day in my dream…

-Hitesh Hinduja.

PERIODIC AUDIT

Let's conduct some basic audit,

And make it as routine periodic,

Destroy what you found toxic,

And live your life exotic,

In the era we believe in robotic,

We are throwing away our profits,

Would you like to talk about this topic?

Far away on country outskirts,

Let's plan a beautiful concert,

Probably by mind will get little divert?

Will speak out what went unheard,

Hope someday someone value my words,

Does it sound like reading a comic?

Would you like to talk about this topic?

We need to set a human alert,

That must be designed by some expert,

It will need some more efforts,

But then everything would be uncensored,

INSIGHT WIZARD

Like the changing minds of perverts,

Emotions will be served stuffed,

I'm now falling sick,

Would you like to talk about this topic?

Changing nature of persons,

Getting away from the closed once,

Living like being in prison,

We are in a bad impression,

Waiting for the end of this session,

Hope this is all an illusion,

Let's together build it brick by brick,

Would you like to talk about this topic?

-Hitesh Hinduja.

INSIGHT WIZARD

I feel like insight wizard,

Take me back to that part,

Where we once played dart,

I still believe in those pieces of art,

I still would love to travel in cart,

Thinking about that time is so fine,

When we all sit together for dine,

I still feel this place is mine,

Give me some hope I will shine,

I do write when words don't rhyme,

Feel the magic that you carry inside,

Live a life with joy and pride,

All we need is peace of mind,

It can be yet little hard o find,

But get back to grind,

Its never too late, you still have time,

You can always be little more kind,

Imagine it the way you want it to be designed,

And the same can be applied,

Be a little more patience, happiness will soon arrive,

You will no longer have to be at fight,

You no longer need emotions to hide,

Finally you be at certain height,

A shinny morning, no more dark nights,

You can now spread your arms wide,

You are free to decide,

You can later even be a perfect guide,

With experience of being soft and wild,

Everyone out will be surprised,

Everything will be same as you described,

You can also feel your inner child,

No more boundaries to be assigned…

-Hitesh Hinduja.

For publisher info

Visit us at

www.fanatixx.in

"SPECTRUM OF THOUGHTS"

- A Unit of FanatiXx.

www.ingramcontent.com/pod-product-compliance
Lightning Source LLC
Chambersburg PA
CBHW051458130726
47987CB00005B/2366